Christine,

all the love and
best wishes,
Bkasey x.

Part One:

The Pier

My name is Evie Jackson.

I am twenty-one years old, and a Gemini.

My mother is an alcoholic waste of space and my father is just a distant memory.

It is 2.30am.

I am sitting on the pier, staring into the dirty river water.

And I am going to die today.

It's a technique called grounding, I've been told. At least, that's what one of the many doctors and therapists told me after I was first diagnosed as a complete, fucking nutcase.

You're supposed to tell yourself things you know; things you can see around you or the smallest sounds you can hear. Supposedly, this will reconnect your worried mind with your body and make you calm again. This

What If?

ISBN: 9781549801600

Imprint: Independently published
Cover Image: LuizClas via Pexels © 2019
Cover Design: B.S. Casey © 2020

Authors Note

This story, while fictional, is a true story for so many people who are struggling with unseen mental illness.

This story is not biographical, but is based on real life experiences and should not be used in place of medical advice, it is just to raise awareness and open a narrative.
If you are dealing with any of the issues addressed in this story, please don't be afraid to seek help, whether professional or a friend.

If you are affected by subjects such as depression, suicide, or substance abuse, please take care when reading.

Stay safe and be kind.

might be the first time it's worked, because I'm calm.

Calmer than I have ever been.

Finally, the days of endless therapy sessions are gone. I don't have to be so scared that I might begin to rattle with the number of pills that I'd been made to shove down my throat. There were your basic anti-depressants and anti-anxiety pills, followed by sleeping pills, pills that were supposed to control my appetite, pills that I couldn't even remember having a use. It's over now.

The crying and screaming in my mind has finally gone away and left peace in its place. I'm sure of myself here, maybe for the first time in forever. I feel a lightness emanating from my chest as I watch the waves go back and forth. I can see each time the pale moonlight bounces onto the ripples in the water, before crashing into the rocks below and quietly retreating.

That exact wave will never form the same way ever again.

It's lost forever, and I was the last one to see it crash into nothingness.

This is the closest thing to happiness I've ever felt.

'Is that how it feels to die?' I ask the air surrounding me.

A giant crash, a crescendo, one final bang and then disappearing into the blackness.

I push my hair from my face, damp and chilly in the mist that is slowly rising and take another mouthful of vodka. I doubt that mum even noticed it was gone. The bitter taste catches in the back of my throat, almost making me gag but I swallow it anyway.

It's warmth.

It's heat.

It's comfort.

I never knew this was where I'd find it.

If I'd worked the timings out right, the tide should be turning soon. Turning away from this nightmare that some people call life. Just a little while longer to wait before the tide will spin away from here and take me with it. The waters will wash away this pathetic excuse of a person I have become and leave no stain of me on this earth. I just need to wait a while longer, and I will be one with the waves, one with the tide.

I will be free.

My most recent therapist asked me once if I'd ever considered taking my own life. I decided to tell her the truth, I don't think it's crossed my mind. I've thought that I didn't want to live, for sure, but hasn't everybody thought that at least once? She told me I needed to think about all of the possibilities that a future would give me. I'd never find out what they were if I wasn't around to see it.

She told me to always think about the 'What If?'. To think about all the things I hope my life will bring and cling to them. That these would give me a reason to keep going.

I tried.

Honestly, I did.

I thought about the possibilities. I didn't even know that I'd wanted to die until I finally noticed what my options in life were.

It had never occurred to me before tonight that this was my only option.

I asked myself, What If?

What if I die right here?

Part Two:

What If I Never Have a Family?

I think I was six years old the first time the screaming woke me up.

Voices.

Anger.

Pain. There was a white noise that I couldn't understand and I didn't want to hear. It forced its way through my ears, all the way into my brain, pounding the whole time.

I hear crashing.

Tables, Chairs, Plates.

Broken, Smashed, Damaged.

The screams got louder, angrier, as I clutched my hands around my duvet, dragging it over my head in a feeble attempt to block out the noise. It felt like it was drowning me. I remember whispering to my tattered old teddy bear to help me, but he didn't answer.

He didn't help.

I threw him across the room, hearing him fall to the floor with a dull thud. I never looked at him again.

It was too much. I muffled a scream, but the pillow couldn't stifle the noise. I forced it over my face, sucking the oxygen out of my body but I couldn't stop screaming. I bit down on my hand, and I felt the skin tear between my teeth, tasted the blood weeping silently from the holes I'd caused. I felt better. I didn't know why, but it helped. Pain.

It stopped the screaming, released the feeling of dread that had built up inside my head, threatening to explode, leaving only traces of my tiny brain.

I sucked in my breath, letting the air rush back into my lungs, and crept out of my bed and down the cold, wooden stairs. We didn't have carpet, so it was always cold. And I always got shouted at if I ever tried to put the central heating on. I was used to the cold now. I was a cold person.

At the bottom of the stairs, I let out a small whimper as I jumped back, clutching my foot. Glass. Broken glass covered the floor.

'Stop being a crybaby!' I told myself as I moved past the danger in the hallway.

I wished I hadn't.

The room was chaos. It was never a nice room, but it was home. We used to play games on the living room table, and curl up on the beaten sofa to watch videos. Sometimes mum and dad would bring home hot chocolate, and we'd sit under a blanket. But this room wasn't home at all.

The dining table was flipped over, the chairs in pieces. Photographs of happier times, of once-smiling faces, lay forgotten on the floor.

The door slammed shut, and I watched as my father left and never came back.

I raise the bottle to my lips once more, a twisted smile playing on my lips. 'This one's for you, Mother', I toast. I hear a car speed past, somewhere in the night behind me. Somebody moving around, living, just existing. Somebody with their own, complete life that I will never know. Who is it? I wonder where they could be rushing off to a 2:45 in the morning? Are they going home? Is it a husband rushing to see his child being born? A criminal running from the police? Someone hurrying to catch a flight, to start their life all over again?

I guess I'll never know.

When you think about how little you really know about the world around you, it makes you feel so small doesn't it?

Five years after my father left, I was hospitalized for the first time.

I was eleven years old. The biting and clawing at myself transformed into an ugly habit, into cutting, and punching. I'd learned to conceal my problems, not as though my mother would have cared if she'd found out.

She used to love me, or at least I think she did. I'm not sure if anybody has loved me. But by now, she hated me. All she did was drink, wake me up so I could nurse her back to a semi-sober state and start drinking all over again. I felt like I was her mother, holding her hair while she cried and vomited, coaxing her to eat some dinner and take a bath. I hated her, too, for acting like this, but I still loved her more than anyone.

She was all I had. She never spoke about her family, all I ever knew is she was an only child and she didn't speak to her parents anymore. I didn't know who my grandparents were, or if I had great uncles and aunts. After a while, I stopped wondering about it. I'd never find out, anyway.

I had no friends, and I didn't blame the other children for not being my friend. I was quiet, shy, and tired. I never had the money to go on the school trips with everyone else. I very rarely had time to make myself a packed lunch and mum didn't always remember to wash my uniform.

I was a reject.

And every laugh at my expense, every shove in the hallways, every terrible name and taunt would manifest itself as another bruise, another scar on my already sick body.

Not as though anyone cared, not even me.

I remember that Christmas was coming up, so of course Mum was at another party. She was probably already drunk and wearing as little as legally possible, on the hunt for the next poor guy that she could leech off for as long as possible before she gets bored.

That year, I was feeling festive for once. I'd managed to dig my way to the back of the cupboard under the stairs and find some old fairy lights that still mostly worked. There was a few old ratty strings of tinsel and baubles in a box. I had convinced myself I could turn the house into a beautiful winter wonderland as I drew pictures of reindeers, angels, and snowmen to hang around the house. I chose the best one, a polar bear running around the snow with tiny elves in the background and wrapped it up in some tin foil. Placing it under the tinselled pot plant I'd used as my little Christmas tree, I'd decided this would be a good day.

The problem is, I was wrong.

So very wrong.

She was supposed to be home at nine, or at least that's what it said on the scribbled note by the front door. Mum was always hungry when she came home, so I decided to make us both dinner. I thought we could sit together around my 'tree' and have a meal together for the first time in years. I didn't really know how to cook very much, I was used to leftovers and microwave pizza, but I figured that pasta was an easy bet. The pan began to boil all over the stove, the sauce spilled all over the counters. It was a mess. I dropped the boiling pan and the pasta fell all over the floor, sizzling on the freezing wood. I tried to mop it up but it seemed to just get messier no matter what I did.

'You stupid kid, what is this?' She screamed, hours later when she finally dragged herself through the front door. She kicked a stray pot across the kitchen floor, her eyes trying to focus on the mess.

Over and over again.

Stupid, Stupid, Stupid.

'Why do you have to try and make my life so difficult? Can't you just let me go out and have fun without causing problems!' She turned to walk away, but not before she started to mutter under the breath, 'I hate this kid sometimes.'

It was so quiet I could have almost missed it, but it felt like she had screamed it at the top of her lungs.

She hated me.

She hates me still.

It's something I'd thought ever since I could remember, but hearing it out loud was something different entirely.

I've never forgotten that moment.

I didn't hear the rest of her mutters, as the tears I didn't want to let out seemed to fill my head, blocking out the slurred curses that were dropping from her lipstick smeared mouth. A few minutes later, she said she was going to the shop to buy cigarettes, slamming the door once again. Why did everybody in this house have to slam doors?

Just like that, I was broken.

I couldn't breathe, my sobs hitching in the back of my throat as my eyes filled with water. Everything was foggy and dark, but my eyes eventually came back into focus on something shiny.

I'd dropped a knife just a few feet away from me. It was nearly as big as my head, wickedly glinting at the edges.

It was gleaming, smooth, dangerous.

And somehow, perfect.

I reached out and let my fingers caress the pointed tip of the blade. I felt like Aurora in Sleeping Beauty, not quite understanding why I was going to prick my finger but just knowing that I needed to touch it.

The pain growing in my chest was uncontrollable. Maybe I wanted a distraction, a new pain to erase the old pain. If I could own it, if I could decide what hurts me, maybe I could be in control of it. I had grown up now. Moved on from broken sharpener blades and scissors, this was something entirely new.

I didn't want to feel the emotions that were forcing their way into my mind anymore. I didn't want to feel.

There was more blood than I had thought I had, seeping its way out of my body, taking the ache along with it. How could such a small person have this much? I didn't know how it would make my head spin, my stomach drop and my knees shake. The pain didn't last that long, but the rush did. I felt everything and nothing all the same time. In and out of the blackness, I could hear the slamming of a door again. I could hear her, louder than ever but I didn't want to listen. She was a background noise, like a fly behind the curtain when you're trying to fall asleep.

'What is wrong with you?', She could have been screaming or whispering, it all sounded the same to me, 'What do you think you're doing, you idiot!'

I know that she slapped me. It should have hurt, but I was okay. I owned my pain now, she couldn't hurt me anymore. I had something that was mine, something that nobody could ever take away from me. I was finally in control.

I stared at her and smirked. 'You're so selfish, why are you doing this? Do you want to make me look like a failure as a mother?' The concern that I could hear coming to the surface wasn't for me at all. That much was clear. She was only worried how it might make her look.

I held her gaze, not finding a trace of care, or fright, or love in her voice. Finally, I focused just enough to tell her something I'd been holding back for years.

'Maybe you are a failure.'

I don't remember what else happened that night, or maybe I just made myself forget. I remember lights, and hospital corridors, long words and lies dripping from my mothers mouth.

Fake concern.

Fake tears.

Fake fake fake. Was anything real about her?

We never spoke about what she said when I was taken to hospital. Actually, we never spoke about that night ever again. I think she wanted to pretend it didn't happen, and I was perfectly fine with that.

Things had changed again.

We spoke on brief occasions when we'd pass on the stairs, or got to the bathroom at the same time. We'd make small talk about the weather during the rare times that we'd actually be in the house at the same time.

She'd leave a card on the table whenever my birthday came and went, but she'd always be in a drunken coma when I'd get up for school and be long gone by the time I'd come home. Sometimes, she'd even remember to leave some money out for dinner or leftovers from whatever late-night fast food joint she'd stumbled into.

To begin with I thought she'd distanced herself from me so suddenly because she felt guilty, because she realised that she'd had a part to play in the way I was. It made sense. Why wouldn't a mother feel responsible for the safety and health of her only child? But over the years I learned an important lesson; she doesn't give a damn.

She was just embarrassed by the thought of me, wondering how much better her life would have been if I'd never been born.

What if she had a better child?

What if I wasn't such a disappointment to her?

What if I'd never been born?

Part Three:

What If I Never Make Friends?

Isla.

I let out a sigh. We used to walk along this river together all the time. Bring a picnic and music, and watch the waves. It's one of the few memories I'm actually fond of.

She was my first friend.

My only friend, if we're being honest about it. The one person that I'd tried to let into my head, to know anything about me. She understood me in a way nobody else could because she was a reject like me.

Long blonde hair, always curled so it was bigger than her head and big blue eyes always covered in glitter and sparkles. She always said she'd draw attention to her face so nobody would notice the little bit of extra weight she was carrying, but I'd never noticed. I thought she was beautiful; the most beautiful girl I'd ever seen before.

I wasn't. I had short, messy hair that stuck up awkwardly as though I had permanent bedhair, and I couldn't even put eyeliner on without looking like a drunk racoon. My body was clumsy and thin, even though it had slowly started to grow some soft edges. I guess I could be pretty if I'd tried to be.

Not as pretty as her, though.

It didn't matter that Isla and I appeared to be polar opposites on the outside, it felt like we were the same person. I was twelve years old, and I had finally made a friend. Isla was in Foster care, she could understand how it felt to be cast out by your own family, how it felt to know that you aren't wanted. She had a few friends, but they weren't really close. They were people to pass the time with, she said, but they weren't real. She couldn't talk to them, confide in them.

It's what brought us together.

I think it was that grieving for families we didn't know that made us become our own family. She invited me over and cooked me dinner that didn't come out of a cardboard box or a plastic tray, for parties and birthdays and even Christmas day. Her foster parents would always remember my birthday, and her mum would always bake me a beautiful cake that would make the house smell like vanilla frosting for days.

There was no place in the world that I'd felt this much love and acceptance.

Before I had Isla, I didn't really have anybody except myself. I'd tried so hard to find anybody, anybody at all who would share their time with me but I never could. When I'd started my new school, I was determined that things would change for me. I was almost certain it would. I'd made sure not to apply to the closest one, because everybody who knew me would be there and I didn't want to spend another five years sitting opposite the same judgmental faces. I wanted to be somewhere new, where nobody really knew me.

Somewhere I could reinvent, maybe.

I was trying to look on the bright side as I put on my newest shirt and polished my shoes so much I thought they might fall apart. I'd managed to tame my hair and felt pretty normal when I looked in the mirror. But what was even better was this flicker of determination that I'd found, a desire to find a place for myself to fit in with anything. I wanted to enjoy myself and try to only worry about stupid things like what I'll wear to prom or what to text a boy like every other girl my age.

And it worked.

It actually worked.

For one day.

One beautiful day.

On my second day of school, I felt sick. But I'd had such a normal day that I was trying to calm the nerves in the back of mind telling me it wouldn't last. I was pushing the black cloud away, hoping that if I shed a little light on it the darkness could clear a little. I felt like maybe there was chance.

I'd managed to chat to a few people in my form room, and actually sat down to eat lunch with a girl from my English Literature class. There was finally a thin strand of hope that I would make it through the next few years as normally as possible. It was a good day, until we got to sports class. We were playing netball, and I was lucky enough to be able to run into a stall and change to avoid any awkward encounters. We could hear the boys shouting from the field where they were playing rugby, and all the girls laughter filled up the building. My team were winning, even though none of us were particularly good at playing.

We high-fived, patted each other on the back, cheered each other on. My head was in the game and in that moment, I didn't think of anything else.

I was just a girl playing a game with her classmates. The ball came my way again, and I was hoping to score again. I rolled up my sleeves, caught the ball and threw it straight into the net. I smiled, waiting for everybody to smile with me once again when I realised what I'd done.

I'd made a mistake.

The game was over for me.

My arms were littered with burns and bruises, like some disgusting painting that nobody would ever want to own. I'd forgotten about them in that singular moment, and that had cost me everything. Nobody said a word, but every person in the room seemed to edge away from me, like they all suspected I had a contagious disease but didn't want to ask. The air between me and them was thick and suffocating, and I was convinced time had stopped and trapped me in this little bubble of awkwardness forever.

I thought I was finally there, I was so close to a shot at normal life that I could almost reach out and touch it with my fingertips. But not now.

My hopes were shattered.

Shattered like picture frames, that lay forgotten on the floor.

Like the feeling of fists against the wall.

I waited for a comment, a laugh, a depreciating joke, but they didn't come. I allowed myself to breathe again, forcing my face to not show the discomfort building in my chest. The game ended, and I'd hoped that the shame and suspense would end with it. It didn't, but I kept telling myself that nobody had noticed. Just minutes later, I'd gotten changed and walked into the hall when it started. Whispers, so quiet that they could have been a figment of my imagination, followed by the looks. These cold, painful stares that felt like pins all over my body. Finally, the laughter came but this time they're weren't laughing with me.

'Hey, Freak!'

I felt my body crash and crumple against the wall, my head bouncing out of the hard brick. The room spun and my temples throbbed as I slid down the wall, tears threatening to flood from eyes and swallow the room like a bad rip-off of Alice in Wonderland. I hear an involuntary moan escape low in my throat as I try to focus through the glaring strip lights above.

They were looking right at me, and I slowly began to understand that I hadn't slipped on the floor and fallen. It was then, the girls from my team. I'd begun to think we could be friends, or at least that I'd be able to walk home from school with them. Just minutes ago, they liked me, but it doesn't take very long for someone to change their opinion of you. I knew that all too well.

I raised my hand to my head as the world became still again and I slowly raised myself up. I wanted to run away and cry, but a spark of anger was burning and it made me want to just combust on the spot.

'What the fuck was that about, you bitch?' I spat at them, just unable to understand why they felt they could push me around. I'd done nothing to these girls, but they decided they'd hated me.

One girl smirked at me, rolling her perfectly lined eyes at her friends who circled around her like a pack. I guess she was the ringleader of this little circus. She edged forward and leaned down slightly to reach my eye-level.

'Aww, you poor little baby,' she said slowly, with a quick look back to her followers, 'I thought you'd be into it, don't you like getting hurt?' The spite in her voice almost dripped from her mouth onto the floor. A ripple of laughter spread through the hallway, connected them all in the misery they were causing me. It joined them together, their hatred for me, but somehow I still couldn't find one thing to connect me with someone else. How did that make sense?

A fist flew out of nowhere and hit me in the stomach, knocking all of the air from my lungs. I didn't have time to recover before someone else stepped forward and pushed me to the floor. I felt so small, so broken that I didn't even fight it. I was too tired to do anything, even when I felt a heavy boot hit the back of my head.

I don't know how long I was laying on the floor, waiting for a teacher or someone to hear their happy screeching and break it up. It could have been just seconds, it could have been hours. I just closed my eyes and held back the tears. I couldn't let them see me cry.

Kayla, who I'd found out later was the girl who'd thrown the first punch was expelled, and I think the others got suspended for a week or so, but it didn't stop a thing.

The trips whenever I'd try to walk up the stairs, the notes left on my desk and the chairs that were pulled out from under me just showed that nothing would change. Every single day, or at least every day I'd muster enough courage to show up, was exactly the same.

And I would have left if it wasn't for Isla.

After yet another incident that mainly involved my face and a wall, I was sitting in the hall outside my school counsellor's office, pretending to read all the quotes plastered in obnoxious neon bubble writing over the off-white walls. They hurt my eyes just to look at them. Almost as much as the overwhelming smell of patchouli seeping from underneath the door. It was meant to create a calm atmosphere in the office but it just gave me a headache.

My face probably looked as hard as the brick it had just slammed into, because I was determined not to break down in front of anybody. I didn't want to talk to anyone, and I was determined that nobody would break my silence. I'd lived this long on my own, what help would they ever be able to offer me?

I didn't notice her to begin with. She might have been sitting opposite me the whole time. Her face was flushed a deep red, streaky lines of mascara staining her cheeks. She was nervously chewing on her bottom lip and holding back tears that had clearly not long ago been running down her face.

She was looking at me.

Looking straight at me, not just through me, wishing I wasn't there like everybody else seems to do. She saw me sitting in front of her and her half of her face lifted in a small smile, like a silent greeting between friends.

'Every single person in here is awful, am I right?'

I took me a moment to register that she was speaking to me. I opened my mouth, willing my brain to find any words to say but this never happened. Nobody ever spoke to me and I didn't know what to do. I nodded slowly instead, not wanting to say something stupid and ruin the first real human interaction I'd had in too long. I wasn't until she glided over to the chairs next to and wrapped her arms tightly around my shoulders that I saw the tears falling onto my lap. She pulled me closer and wiped away a single tear that was lingering on my cheek.

I tried to force the tears to stop, choking them back and look at this girl who was being so kind to me.

'I'm sorry!', I managed to make myself say, wondering why she was putting up with me being like this around her, let alone comforting me. Was this some type of sick joke? Was she waiting for me to talk so she could laugh about me later?

She did laugh, but it was such an amazing sound. It was happy, beautiful and full of life. It made her face light up and her smile reached all the way up into her bright eyes.

'Don't you ever apologise to me for crying, okay?' She leaned and closed the gap between us, lowering her voice so that her words for me alone, 'Don't ever let anybody make you feel like you need to be sorry for feeling. They don't deserve it, you got that?'

Her words got into my head, they reached me. After all this time waiting, somebody had finally managed to break through. She started talking, introducing herself, and I was quite happy to sit there and listen to the sound of her voice. It was delicate, soothing and melodic. She was waiting for the counsellor too, because she had found out just how cruel people could be here.

She told me about how she was given up as a baby and had jumped between foster homes most of her life, but now she's found something she calls her 'Forever Family'. Both words felt foreign on my lips.

'You are not a weak person because you're sitting here. I need help too, and trust me when I say having to admit that to myself was the toughest thing I've ever done. I still see the shrink here every week just to make sure I'm still on the right track, you know? Everybody needs to vent once in a while, and when there are people who need to bully anybody they can, it makes sense. People might think that because I'm not thin, or because I don't live with my biological parents that I'm less than they are. But it doesn't mean that at all. I don't think so anyway, so why should I care what these idiots think?'

I listened to her monologue go on, and slowly she began to make sense.

'But how did you find the strength?' I asked her, 'To admit you needed help.'

She sighed, looking into my eyes, 'You need to decide that you're worthy of it first. And I think you are.'

She walked me home after I'd made my appointment with the counsellor, and as we walked down the pavement together she wound her arms through mine as though we'd been best friends for our whole lives.

She really was my best friend, a ray of light and hope that somehow would break through the imaginary grey clouds that were constantly raining over my head. She was the only person in the world that knew me, and loved me regardless of any reason that she shouldn't.

But it was too good to last. I lost her too, in time.

What if I never get my best friend back?

What if I never make another friend?

Part Four:

What If I Keep Getting My Heart Broken?

3.15 am.

You can see the water shift and turn. It's mesmerizing. In, and out, it's a constant. You can always rely on the turn of the tides, and it is the one thing left in this world that I trust. It's almost time, I can feel my heart racing, picking up the pace in time with the waves.

My heart races now, but for a while, it just didn't work. It hasn't worked in years. I've loved four people in my whole life: My Father, and my Mother for a while, Isla, and Liam. I hiss when I think of that name, shaking my head as though I could shake the memory of him from my mind.

I met him on the last day of school, my final day in that hell I'd spent five long, hellish years in. I and Isla had had lunch together in our favourite cafe and skipped off to school to get our exam results. Isla had passed everything with flying colours, just like I knew she would. She held my hand as I opened the envelope that decided my future.

I'd passed everything.

Not as well as Isla, but I'd passed. I didn't think I had a hope in hell, and if it wasn't for her helping me study every night I would have failed every single question. But this was yet again some type of hope, I could go to college, and I could start over once more. But this time, I was going to start again with my best friend right beside me.

I'd applied to study Creative Writing. I spent a lot of my time in therapy, writing about how I felt. But I didn't do diary entries, that just wasn't me. I wrote it in poems, and in stories. I wrote about little girls, lost in a storm, in a small boat that couldn't fight the crushing waves. But sometimes, I'd write about sunlight, and flowers, and every now and then, happiness.

In that moment, I felt like I could write a whole book about happiness. Isla went off to the careers department, to talk about getting ready for college and I stayed around to wait for her.

That's when he came over. We'd sat together in English for the last year, and while he wasn't friendly to me, he wasn't exactly nasty either. He'd never said anything to taunt me or hurt me, just kept an indifference towards to me throughout the time we'd known each other.

'How'd it go?' He asked, running his hands through his spiky black hair. He had the type of hair you could tell took ages to get right every day. I didn't answer at first, till he cleared his throat and moved a little closer.

'Oh! Sorry, were you talking to me?' He smiled, bemused, as he nodded at me.

I raised my envelope in my hand awkwardly, shrugging my shoulders. 'I did okay. I got good enough grades to get into college.' I spoke calmly, not wanting to show the pathetic excitement bubbling up inside my stomach. He smiled at me, it was a bright smile, it made me happy just looking at it. He raised his hand up and placed it on my shoulder, looking into my eyes.

'Well done, Evie, right?'

How did anybody even remember my name around here? Nobody called me by my name. Nobody ever cared enough to ask for it.

'Thanks' I trailed off, realised I'd not remembered his name. I think I blushed, and I stuttered, looking for something to say.

'My names Liam, by the way. Just in case you forgot.' He didn't look mad I'd forgotten. He was still smiling, and he stayed that way right until Isla came back for me, waving at me and Liam with a glow on her face, and she giggled as she dragged me away. She'd been gone for nearly half an hour, but it felt like she'd just walked out the door seconds ago.

I looked back.

The next week, Isla went on holiday with her family. She was only gone for two weeks, but it killed me every second she was away. I cried like a baby when I went to the airport with her, and the entire train ride home. I didn't know how I could cope without her. Checking the exit was clear from guards, I jumped over the ticket barrier and smoothly walked out of the building and onto the high street, hoping I wouldn't get caught. I don't know why I worried, I'd never been caught before. I was invisible to most people.

The next thing I knew; I was on the floor again. I held my breath and waited for the kicking and screaming to start, but instead, someone held out their hand and helped me up. It was Liam. He let go of my hand and cleared his throat, brushing my messed up hair from my eyes.

'Fancy bumping into you here!' He said to me, and I just looked at him. 'Okay, that was a bad joke, I know. But are you okay? I didn't knock you too hard did I, I wasn't looking where I was going.'

'No! I'm fine, honest. Thanks for helping me up.'

He nodded at me, taking a pack of cigarettes from his shirt pocket, and placed one gently against his lips. I'd never looked at his lips before, they were interesting to stare at. He lit it and inhaled, his chest rising and falling with the smoke. He extended the pack to me and I took one, placing it against my lips like he did before he leaned over and lit it for me.

I'd never smoked before. The first breath felt like my lungs were on fire, searing down my throat. But I tried again, and it felt better. Taking a deep breath, blowing out the smoke and watching it play in the air. We smoked in silence for a while, until he turned back to me and said, 'You hungry?'

I was starving, but I just said, 'I suppose so.' He wrapped his arm around mine, letting his warm skin graze against mine and told me he was taking me for lunch. I didn't have a chance to say no before he led me into a cosy French deli on the other side of the street. We sat on the sofa in the corner and ordered hot chocolates, looking at the menus. I don't remember what we had, we were talking so much I didn't know how we managed to find the time to eat a thing.

I noticed things I'd never seen before. His hand would cover mine or reach out and touch my thigh, which was leaning comfortable against his. He would look right at me, listening to everything I said. Being interested in me, laughing at my jokes.

'Hey what are you doing tomorrow?' He asked me, as we stepped outside into the street, which had already turned dark while we'd been talking. I told him, I was doing nothing. But that wasn't new.

'Fancy hanging out again? I had a good time with you.' He was close to me; I could feel his breath on my face. I nodded at him, still in disbelief that another person would want to spend time with me two days in a row.

'I'd like that' It was almost a whisper. 'What time?' I said, a little bit louder.

He kissed me.

His hands cupped my face, and pulled me to him, in a silent question. Then before I knew it, his lips were on mine. They were soft, and he tasted like coffee and cigarettes. His lips opened mine, drawing me into him as his hands slipped down to my waist, holding me tightly against him.

We pulled apart, breathing heavily and lips bruised, as wrote his number on my hand and bid me goodnight. 'Call me tomorrow?'

I called. We spent the next two weeks' side by side, every day. It was bliss. We went for lunch, took a walk in the park, all that cliché summer romance shit you see in all the movies. We kissed, we held hands, we held each other closer than anybody had held me before. He told me I was beautiful and intelligent and amazing. I almost believed him.

I hadn't asked if we were dating, I was so scared he would leave and never speak to me again if I pushed him. But it was the day before Isla was coming home, and I wanted to introduce them. I knew she'd be so happy for me. Liam had made a picnic, and I was more than shocked when I saw everything I liked in the little basket, all the things I'd told him I'd liked.

His arm was draped around my shoulders, his head resting on mine. We'd been talking about nothing and everything all day, just bringing anything up to stall what I really needed to say. I knew I didn't have long till I had to go home, so I reigned in all my courage and came out with it all at once.

'Liam are we dating or something? It looks like we are but you haven't said if you want to or not so,' His lips cut me off, with a quick kiss. He sighed and rubbed the back of his neck awkwardly, looking away. I knew something was wrong.

'Well then. I'd best be going.' I pulled myself from under his arms but he reached out and took my hand, imploring me to stay.

'Evie,' He said, his voice low and sad, 'I want to be with you. You're the most amazing girl I've ever met. But it's complicated right now.'

I barked a bitter laugh, 'Complicated? Could you give a more typical excuse?'

'Look, it's not an excuse, I promise.' He let go of my hand and looked at the ground next to him. I cautiously sat down. 'I know I should have said something sooner, but I was having so much fun with you I just didn't want to ruin this, you know?'

'Could you please get on with it?'

'I have a girlfriend.'

Four words that hurt me for the first time. But I was naive, and that's how I managed to forgive him and allow myself to get hurt again. He explained he had a girlfriend, but he didn't want to be with her anymore. He promised he would leave her because he wanted me.

I wanted someone to want me. So I forgot all about it, kissed him goodbye and texted Isla to find out when to meet her at the airport the next day.

She was tanned, beautiful and happy when she came out of the gate and ran towards me. She had braided her hair so that it swung around my shoulders as she hugged me. I'd missed her so much. She told me all about her trip and I listening in awe, wishing I could have been there to have adventures with her. She promised me we'd have our own adventures one day.

We got back to her house, throwing the suitcases straight onto the floor and collapsing in a tired heap on the carpet. It felt like coming home, whenever I was with her. Her foster mother, Ella, came in and said she'd have to pop out. Her own mother wasn't feeling too well and needed a hand at home, which was about a six-hour drive away.

'But mum!' Isla whined, 'I thought we were having a celebration tonight?'

She'd mentioned that they were having some friends over to celebrate Isla getting into college, and she looked so upset that it hurt my head. Ella pursed her lips, and rolled her eyes.

'Fine!' She held her hands up, 'You can still have your friends over, just don't cause trouble and have everyone gone at a reasonable time though, okay?'

Isla jumped and grabbed her mum, 'Thank you! We'll be good, I promise!'

Ella kissed her on the top of the head, 'I know you will. We'll be back tomorrow afternoon and we'll take you out for dinner to make it up to you. Sorry honey.'

She walked out the room, and as soon as we heard the door close we fell into fits of laughter.

'House party! Yes!'

I was so excited. We'd never had a party without her parents being there, never been to a real house party and I was sure this would be amazing. I'd talk to her friends, I'd make them like me and I'd make friends before I went to college. Nothing could bring me down.

Ella left us some money to get snacks and said we could take a few bottles of wine from the cellar, as long as we were careful. We'd drunk a few glasses with dinners through the years, it made us feel grown up, how sad is that?

Isla had called up her friends, told them to bring their friends and we head out to get party supplies. We were in the supermarket, and we'd split up to find everything. I'd got everything on my list so I'd wandered happily back to the snack aisle to find Isla. She was smiling coyly, her phone pressed to the side of her face as she whispered into it. She turned around to me, biting her lip and laughing. She looked like the child with her hand in the sweetie jar.

'Okay, gotta go. Love you. Bye!' She whispered sweetly.

'And who was that exactly, miss!' I said, grabbing her hand, watching the happiness dance around her face.

She slipped her phone back into her jeans, and stared at me, shaking her head.

'Okay, so I've wanted to say something for a while now. I'm seeing someone!'

'Isla why didn't you tell me? That's amazing!' I was so happy for her, she had never had a real boyfriend before and she really deserved someone to love her. Someone to spoil her and treat her like the beautiful woman I know she is.

'Sorry!' She drawled, 'I just didn't tell anyone yet. It's been a secret; I was going to tell you soon but I might as well tell you about it now! We've been together a few months now, he's just amazing.' She switched, looking a bit awkward now, 'Just don't tell mum, you know she's funny about me dating anybody so I'm keeping it a secret for now.'

'Why don't you invite him tonight? I need to meet your mystery man!'

'Of course! I didn't even think of it. Oh, Evie, you are the best. You'll just love Liam.'

My heart stopped. Everything was in slow motion. Liam?

It couldn't be my Liam, could it? It was such a common name; it could be anyone. But he did say he had a girlfriend. I had to find out.

'Liam? Oh! Is that the one that I met after the last day of school?'

She nodded and it suddenly clicked. Why she came over to me and Liam looking so happy, giggling as we walked away from him. Liam was dating my best friend.

'That's great, Isla. I can't wait to meet him properly.' I forced out the words, hoping I was convincing enough. I suppose I was because we carried on shopping and left to get ready.

She ransacked her wardrobe, picking out a beautiful black dress for me to wear. It hung halfway down my thighs, with straps all the way down the back. It was so pretty. If only I had someone to look pretty for. She looked gorgeous though, but she always did to me. She had a shocking pink A-line dress on, that made her curves look something from a pin-up magazine.

'You look amazing, Is. No wonder you got a boyfriend!' I said, as sincerely as I could muster. She was curling her hair as I sat on the other side of the room putting on some make-up. I saw tears well in the corners of my eyes before I even felt them.

She was looking at me, mouth wide open and half covered in lipstick.

'Are you alright?' She said gingerly.

I wiped my eyes, nodding far too enthusiastically 'Just got a bit of mascara in my eyes. Stings like a bitch, but I'm okay!'

I wasn't okay. I was far from okay. I'd trusted Liam. I'd cared about him, I'd spent time with him, I'd started to fall in love with him. I didn't quite believe it, though. I refused to believe it until I saw him. He'd be holding her hand, like he did with me. Kissing her, like he kissed my lips just yesterday. Would he brush her hair from her face the same way? Would he caress her the same way?

Would he hurt her the same way?

I knew right then; I should have told her. I wanted to tell her, but how could I? I couldn't lose her over him, and I didn't want her to live with the fact her first boyfriend had cheated on her. I couldn't lose Liam and Isla on the same day. I couldn't handle it.

He turned up just after 9 pm. The party was going fine, I was starting to relax after having a few glasses of wine and actually managing to talk to a few of her friends. That's when he came in. The room seemed suddenly suffocating, smaller than before. I found some more wine and almost threw it down my throat, watching him crack open a can of cheap beer and wrapping his arms around my best friend, just like he'd done to me a few days ago.

Her face was pure happiness. She looked up at him as though he was a guardian angel, resting her head against him and drinking in her bliss. How could I really take that away from her?

How could he?

As they walked over, I refilled my once again empty glass and plastered a fake smile onto my face, extending my hand to the boy I was supposed to be a stranger to.

'Nice to properly meet the guy who's made my best friend so happy!'

He paused, for almost a second, a look of worry shooting across his near-perfect face as he shook my hand, falling into an endless stream of small talk and merriment. He told me how he'd spent his last couple of weeks camping with his friends, having some break where conveniently they try and live with any proof; I mean technology the whole time they're away. It was a good cover.

The time passed slowly, it was almost midnight but it felt like days had passed and my face was hurting from trying to keep my lips up and my act from breaking. I walked up to Isla's room and crashed onto the bed, throwing my shoes onto the floor and drinking straight from the bottle. My head was spinning and I didn't feel connected to my body anymore. I'd never been really drunk before, but I guess this was how being drunk felt. I liked it. I rolled onto my side to look out the window and I heard the door open softly behind me, my peace disturbed.

'What the fuck do you want, Liam? 'I whispered, my voice not carrying in the stale air. He smelled as though he used his beer as an aftershave, and his face was slowly getting red. He sat next to me, placing his hand on my arm but I shrugged him off. But instead of letting me go, he grabbed me and turned me so my face was just inches from his.

'I'm sorry' Those two words hit me in the chest, and as his lips met mine again my mind became blank and all I could feel was him and me. My heart was beating so badly I thought it was going to jump out of my throat, and I shivered as he deepened the kiss. I felt him sigh happily into my mouth. It felt right, just like it had all along with him. I wanted him to want me, and he did. I should have known he would come back to me; how could you fake the feelings we'd had this whole time?

His chest against mine, his hands in my hair, running down my back. My clothes fell to the floor as he kissed me, and I watched in amazement as he took off his shirt, like it was some type of crazy dream that I didn't ever want to wake up from.

But I woke up.

Naked, Scared, and just having lost my virginity to my best friend's boyfriend. We lay side by side, entangled in one another and breathing heavily, but I went cold. I froze. I could feel his fingers running through my hair and his touch made me feel sick. I felt it like a mark on my entire body, a mark I didn't think would ever scrub off. I could feel his chest moving, his breathing becoming steady as he fell into a happy sleep.

How could he sleep? Didn't he realise what we'd just done?

I peeled myself from him, watching as he muttered in his sleep and rolled away from me, as I tried to piece together the items of clothes I'd left scattered across the floor. I looked in the mirror and saw a girl I didn't know. Red face, messy hair, smudged makeup and a look of utter revulsion on her face.

But the one face that was worse was hers.

Isla's face as she stood in the open doorway still kills me to think about. She had one of Liams' cigarettes resting against her lips, tears streaming down her cheeks and onto her lips. She looked right through me, as though I'd suddenly stopped existing.

Her heart was broken, and so was mine. I'd lost them both, and everything was broken.

What if my heart just keeps breaking?

Part Five:

What If the Shame Never Goes Away?

I've reached that point when you know you've drunk a bit too much, but you don't really care about it. It's too late to do anything about it so might my stomach spikes up every now and then, leaving an acrid taste in the back of my throat which I just wash away with another mouthful of vodka. My head is spinning like the earth spins around and around, constantly. Everything starts to feel like a wonderful blur, and if I stop paying attention my eyes stop focusing and everything starts to pixelate into lights, and colours, and nothing at all.

'Nothing at all. Nothing at all. Nothing at all.'

I say it over and over, letting the words roll over my tongue. It's comforting, isn't it? If there's nothing at all, there's no pain, no sadness, no anger. Nobody to disappoint and nobody left to disappoint you. Nobody at all, and I'm better off that way.

My first day at college wasn't like my first day at a new school. I didn't convince myself that I'd have a brand new start, or a bright future ahead of me, I was beyond believing anything like that was possible for me. I walked in on that first day with a closed off face, clutching my second-hand books in my hand like a vice. I saw my knuckles whiten and tried to relax, not even realizing my hands were aching. I had a plan; go to college, learn about books, and sit in the library until they had to physically remove me. If I just repeated that every day, I'd get through this.

I found my registration room and sat in the far corner, looking out the window into the browning athletics field, trying to draw the least attention to myself as humanly possible. I tried to sneak a quick glance around the room, trying to find out who I'd be seeing every morning for the next two years. I didn't recognize the faces as I scanned the room until the small cluster of students next to door looked back at me. They'd all been in my old school, they'd all seen me freak out, and break down, and listened and laughed as people talked about what happened over the summer.

Well, probably. I don't know how much these people actually did, but I can't imagine that anybody at that cursed school didn't know every detail about me. One of them, a girl I think I'd spoken to briefly, about three years ago, looked over to me and I made the mistake of catching her eye. She looked straight through me, but I could tell she recognized me as she smirked and turned back to whisper to her friends. Things never change, do they?

And for once, things really didn't change. The next sixth months went by in the routine I'd planned. I went to college, after checking my mother and whatever hungover prick she was with were still breathing and kept to myself. I'd speak casually to people I studied with, and some of them I actually liked to speak to, even if it was only just about the next essay we handed in, which was better than talking about me. During lunch, I'd go the library and do my homework, and after college I'd go back for a few hours, silently thanking whatever Gods were out there that it opened a few hours after lessons end.

When I couldn't stall any longer, I'd take a slow walk home.

Mother wasn't home much, but when she was we'd make small talk and sometimes she'd order us dinner. She asked about college, I asked about her newest manicure or her shoes, anything to fill up the awkward silence before it was an acceptable time to go to bed and start the routine all over again.

It may sound boring, it bores me just thinking about it, but it was perfect. It was Nothing.

I saw Liam once, in passing, the one time I went to the canteen but I walked off without even getting anything. I couldn't deal with having to share air with that boy, or the new blonde draped adoringly over him. I actually smiled to myself when I saw that, glad that Isla hadn't stayed with a terrible person like that. Part of me wanted to see her, just to look at her from across a classroom, but she was in a different building and always went off-site for lunch. So I hadn't so much as glanced at her yet, but I knew she was here.

Just like Liam knew I was here.

And I didn't realize, but he was going to make sure everybody knew I was here.

It started slowly, the deathly stares and the silence when I'd walk by like it always did. But I'd tried to accept things like that by now. It was as natural as breathing for me. Then came the sudden silence when I walked into a room, and the hushed tones punctuated by frequent glares in my direction. But when he started showing up everywhere I looked, I knew I wasn't being paranoid. I wasn't just expecting people to judge me, to talk about every time my back was turned, it was really happening again. I couldn't figure it out, I was so careful this time. I always wore long sleeves, I didn't cry or freak out until I got home and was tucked away in the solitude of my own bedroom.

He'd be there when I left classes, casually leaning against the wall outside. He'd be there when I'd run off to the toilet to breathe for five minutes. He'd be there when I left, waiting by the path I'd take to go home. And every single time I saw him, he would have a dirty smile on his wretched face, looking right through me. He'd raise an eyebrow, challenging me to say something, to acknowledge his presence, but I'd just look straight ahead and walk a little faster.

I'd hoped I'd made it look like he didn't faze me, but he did. I'd get home and panic, expecting him to be at my door, or under my bed, or even behind the shower curtain. I'd cry until I couldn't breathe until I felt my lungs ache with the lack of oxygen and my throat tighten with the pain of trying to keep my sobs silent. I'd punch at the concrete of my walls, watching my bloody, bruised knuckles leave red stains on the wall. I'd imagine his skin, as I scratched at my own arms and legs, wishing he'd understand the pain he had caused me.

I'd say I was over it, over him and what he'd done to me.

But I wasn't.

He'd reminded me that I was alone and that I couldn't trust anybody. That nobody would love me. A fact I would try every day to convince myself wasn't true. But, I still put on that brave face. I could not let people see the mess that living right behind my eyes. I didn't slip up.

Until the day before Easter half term. It was almost the end of an entire year of college. I'd just finished cramming for my first exam and I really needed coffee. I walked over to the canteen to buy myself the biggest black coffee I could find when I finally saw it. Liam was sitting on a table, his friends flocking around him as always, laughing maniacally, all staring at me. Not through me this time, right at me. And there, on the back of all their folders was a photograph.

Of me. Drunk, naked, and ruining my life.

Liam winked at me, and I lost it. I screamed, knocking them as I ran past. I didn't notice who I'd bumped into along the way as I sprinted through the halls, tears dripping down my exposed face. I burst into my empty classroom to snatch my bag, and there, on top of a folder, was another picture. I ripped it into shreds, throwing it into the air as I threw my chair into the air, hearing it slam to a halt against the wall. I pulled at my hair, trying to own my own breathing for even a moment. I could see a crowd from the corner of my eye, gathering eagerly outside the door, ringside seats to a private freak show. My shaking hands reached to grab my phone and keys, but as I went to throw them into my pockets I saw the text messages. I had almost a hundred. Picture after picture, from numbers I'd never seen. Every single person, rubbing salt into a wound that I'd left to rot. I heard screaming and crying, an unnatural, painful sound but by the way, everyone stared I realized it was me. I couldn't hear it over the noise inside my head.

My legs gave way as I kicked and I punched the floor below me, not being able to see the tears and drops of blood that trickled onto the dirty carpet below.

'Get away from the door!' I'm sure I heard somebody shout, and I felt somebody enter the room and edge their way onto the floor beside me. 'Evie?' The voice said carefully, 'We're going to clear this hall, and I'd like you to come with me. Can you stand?' The voice asked me how badly hurt I was, told me over and over I was going to be okay now, they would help me. Inside, I laughed at the thought that somebody thought I was even capable of being helped.

The next morning, they let me out of the hospital on the agreement that I'd be in intensive therapy. I didn't really know what happened the night before, apart from being prodded and poked by doctors. My hands were bandaged, and there was a giant plaster on the side of my face, I suppose I hurt it when I fell. My mum picked me up with a simple, 'Are you feeling okay now?' and a mention of getting pizza for dinner. Everything felt like a dream, just gliding from moment to moment, unsure of how I got there.

When I finally climbed into my own bed, I read the letters I'd been given. My teacher had found me, and taken me to the hospital, telling them I'd had a mental breakdown of sorts. There were words I didn't understand, but I got the subtext of the letter - I'm crazy. I let my eyes wander to the bottles of tablets that were sitting on my table. I emptied them onto my bed, wondering how anybody thought a few coloured tiny pills would help me. I tried to remember what they said; One of these before you go to bed, it'll help you sleep. Three of every day, they'll help control your depression, and should make you feel better.

I swallowed one of each, not feeling them as they worked their way through my body. I waited to feel something, looking at my darkened reflection on the window to see if I'd changed. But all I saw was the bruised, puffy-faced girl that I'd seen the day before. I looked at the girl in the reflection, into her eyes, hoping I'd see the shame in her eyes fade and a glimmer take its place.

But it didn't.

What if this feeling never goes away?

What if this is it for me?

Part Six:

What If I Never Work Again?

 In case you didn't already guess, I never stepped foot in that college again. I hadn't seen anybody from my time as a student in about two years now, and that was just fine with me. They probably missed me just as much as I missed them.

It was my nineteenth birthday, and my therapist, Natalie, had brought me in a cupcake, which was probably against all the rules in the book. My therapy sessions were only once a week by then, rather than the daily torture I had to go through after college. She was actually a pretty nice person; I think she was in her mid-30's or so. She had light, wispy blonde hair and bright eyes that could always tell when I was lying to her. Those eyes always looked so hopeful, so sure that I would recover, so much that sometimes I'd even believe her for a moment.

Natalie took a lighter out of her pocket and lit a little purple candle resting on the cake, holding out towards with as she told me to make a wish. I looked up at her and attempted a smile as I closed my eyes and blew out the flame.

'Thank you, Natalie.' I said, trying to sound as polite I could. I never knew what to do when people did things for me. I hesitated, then added, 'Mum remembered to get me a card this year, so that's pretty good. She even stayed and made me a sandwich before I came here.'

'Well, that's something, Evie. I'm happy she remembered this time.' She said, busying her hands making us both a coffee. She sat down on the other fluffy armchair and flicked open her folder, reading the notes from the last weeks meeting. We talked about all the usual things she had to check; how much I'm eating or sleeping, if the pills are giving me any side-effects, if I'd hurt myself at all. I lied to her about it at first, but she always knew. I'd tell her about every single day without food, about every single night I cried myself to sleep and every single scar I'd inflicted on myself. I felt like I could tell her. She cared, but not too much that I'd feel awful for burdening her with my problems.

I tried to force my legs to stop twitching as I tried to get comfortable, my nerves basically screaming out at Natalie. I didn't even need to say anything; she knew what it was that was annoying me so much.

'Look, you'll find a new job. Some people don't understand mental illnesses and they don't know how to deal when their staff are dealing with them. I know you've had a hard time but we'll help you do something about it, okay?'

I nodded, taking a sip of my coffee. After I was given the okay after my major breakdown, I tried to find work. I couldn't take sitting indoors, staring at the ceiling and the walls while my mind replayed things I just didn't want to think about. I'd got a job in a coffee shop, but lost that after I just couldn't focus one day. A while later, I tried working in a book store, which sounded like heaven to me but after I started crying whenever I had angry customers, it seemed better than I left. I'd tried a few more jobs here and there but they never lasted.

'Remember the What If, Evie. What if you find a job you love? What if this all works itself out?' She said in a heartbreakingly optimistic voice. Natalie loved the What If Game, it was too bad I'd taken my own spin on it.

When it was finally the end of the session, I walked down one of the many high streets, filled with people getting on with their lives, not even noticing me. Sometimes, a busy street could actually be the best place to hide. I passed a few stores, and the smell of disgustingly greasy fast food filled my nose, making my stomach do a backflip. God, I was hungry. The pretty cupcake was in my bag, but I didn't want to eat it, so I pressed my face against the window looking at all the food I knew I couldn't really afford to get seeing as I was yet again unemployed.

As I scoured the bright neon menu on the wall, I saw a poorly handwritten sign for a vacancy in the corner, taped around the edges. I wasn't exactly the place for a career goal, but I needed to do something so I went inside and asked the large man behind the counter if I could apply. He had a thick, deep accent that was hard to understand but I smiled and nodded along as he finally said

I could come in and try out the next day. I didn't shake his hand; I don't think I would have ever got the smell off. I turned on my heel and walked back into the fresh air, not thinking too much about how much I'd need to wash my hair if I started working in that greasehole. Mentally preparing myself for the day ahead, I lost myself in my own head for a while until I reached the road and tried to bring myself back to earth. I looked along the curb, finding a place to cross ... but then I froze.

Standing only a few meters away from me was Isla. My best friend. I still called her that because she was my best and only friend, whether I was hers anymore or not. She looked amazing as if she'd got even more beautiful since the last time I'd seen her. It made my heart ache, and then stop as she stepped towards me, with a determined face.

'Look, Evie, I...' She began to speak, closing the distance between us with clenched fists, and there was no doubt in my mind she had half a mind to crush me into the road. But she didn't get the chance.

'No, Isla!' I cried out, her name like acid on my tongue, 'I know I deserve it but I just can't. I can't!' I was almost screaming as I turned away from her, falling onto the concrete and feeling my nose break against the path. I scrambled to my feet, gripping my bloody face as I ran home, hearing her voice linger behind me. I didn't listen, I couldn't do it. I forced my shaking hands to grab my keys and let me into the house, almost collapsing once I was finally through the door. I steadied my breathing, wiping my face as I heard my mum coming down the stairs.

'Shit, what happened?' She asked, a bit too casually, ripping off some kitchen paper and handing it to me. I held it against my face and nodded a thank you. Once I could breathe again, I began to mention Isla's name and she held up her hand.

'Say no more, that's gotta sting.' She walked around me, into the kitchen came out a few moments later with a bottle of gin and two glasses. 'Drink?

She passed out somewhere around two in the morning, during the second bottle. Of course, the way to get her attention was to drink with her, how didn't I figure that out sooner? She asked me about therapy, but still cringed when I began to actually talk about myself as a patient, so I stopped talking about it and let her talk instead. Halfway through telling me about some new man she was drooling over, she actually started drooling as she slumped into her chair and started snoring. I poked her, but she was out cold, so I slipped the bottle from her fingers and filled up my glass, jumping as my phone buzzed with a pill reminder. I rolled my eyes as I tried to lift myself from the sofa, feeling my legs liquefy beneath me and the room begins to roll around. I made my way to abandoned back, and carefully extracted my 'happy pills', staring at it as I moved it around my hand.

Was I happy? I didn't feel much of anything then.

I didn't want to think about it, so I swallowed the pill and swallowed my questions as me and my bottle of Gin curled up in bed, popping some of mums stupid romcoms into my centuries old television.

These stupid films were much more tolerable when paired with a good drink. I didn't notice how much time I'd wasted staring gormlessly at the screen until my alarm went off, sending my flying into the air.

It was time to wake up and get ready for work. My head was still spinning, but I took a deep breath and willed myself to stay together for a few hours, just to make it past one little lunch shift and then I could come home and pass out. I quickly showered, imagining the water washing away nausea that was rising up inside me. I tried to put on a bit of makeup but my hands wouldn't stop shaking and I ended up looking like a raccoon so I just washed my face again and set off down the road.

The sun burned my eyes, all the way to my brain. My whole body ached and I was shaking as though it was the middle of winter, but I managed to walk the whole way back to the greasehole without much of a problem. It was 11 am, and all I could think about was turning around and sleeping for the next few days, but I kept going. It's just a few hours, I told myself, a few hours and you can sleep.

I knocked on the door as the giant man pulled it open, and that's all I can remember about my first and only day at that job until I woke up on a dirty tiled floor.

It was cold and slippery with grease, the cheap strip lights above me made my eyes ache. 'Maybe you should go home now.', a man said to me as I lifted myself precariously from the floor. Blinking my surroundings back into focus, I saw that it was my very large boss. I hadn't even asked his name; it didn't seem that important at the time.

'I'm fine now, sorry...' I began to try and apologise but the counter I'd try to lean on was further than I had expected so I crumpled back to the floor like the pile of rubbish stacked in the corner. 'I think it's time for you to go home now, miss. There's no need to worry about coming back for your shift.' And just like that, I'd failed before I even got started.

I look at the bottle in my hand, trying to pinpoint exactly when I fell so far off the rails. I was like a train that slipped off the tracks, destroying everything it comes into contact with. I pull my jacket tighter around my body, staving off the early morning chill that was setting into my bones as duck under the metal railings and move myself closer to the edge of the pier, dangling my legs off the edge like a child on a set of swings. I look around, making sure nobody saw me sneak to the edge. I've heard of a few kids getting taken away by the police for trespassing here, but how stupid do you have to be to get caught in a place with no security cameras or lighting? Pretty stupid, I guess.

'I don't know what happened!', I screamed at Natalie, 'I've drunk more than that before, but I've never lost control of my own legs! I looked like a complete nutcase!

I...'. My words failed me as I threw myself onto the chair, curling my arms around my knees.

'Evie', she said softly, leaning towards me, 'I don't want to sound condescending, but have you drunk this much since you started taking your new medication?'

'Of course, I have!' I retorted back to her, but then a party started in front of my eyes. I was wearing a pretty dress, drunk out of my mind, and somebody was kissing me, taking my pretty dress away and throwing it into a heap on the floor. Then of a beautiful blonde girl, her face wet with tears and she raised a cigarette to her lips. 'I don't know. After the whole thing with Liam I've always tried to make sure I don't get wasted, just a little tipsy when I need to relax.' '

Do you remember the meeting we had when you first tried out your pills? About side effects?', she was trying to edge me softly into the conclusion that I'd done this to myself, and I suddenly realised it was my fault. I thought back to hazily reading through pages of health warnings and side effects, specifically about drinking while medicated. If consumed with alcohol, can cause dizziness, disorientation, and depression. I remember reading it, but instead of taking it in I laughed at the idea of an anti-depressant making me depressed. I shook my head, dumbfounded at just how stupid I'd been; this had been explained to me time and time again. Everybody knew you shouldn't drink when you're on any pills, but I guess I was already drunk before my common sense could actually see it.

This stupid mistake cost me a job. Admittedly a pathetic, dead-end job but still one of the only places in a ten-mile radius I hadn't already been fired from. This medicine had ruined everything for me. I knew Natalie was talking, but I didn't hear a word she was saying, I just nodded when it seemed appropriate. I just watched her lips as they moved, but nothing came out of them until I saw her mouthing words I noticed.

'Sorry, what was that?' I asked, trying to sound as though I'd at least been half-listening.

'Your phone is buzzing; I think it's pill time. Maybe without the side of Gin this time.' She tried to be playful, make me feel like it wasn't a big deal. But what did she really know? She'd studied me, but she didn't know me. She was a watching me apprehensively as I reached for my bag, taking the strip of pills as I popped one out and brought it to my lips. I willed myself to swallow it, just like I should of. But my throat began to close up and my mouth had gone dry, and the pill just stayed beneath my tongue.

Finally, time was up for another week and Natalie put her hand on my shoulder, smiling sadly in some attempt to reassure me I'd be perfectly fine. I just smiled back, as well as I could and told her I'd see her next week. Once I was out of sight, I spat the pill into my hand, and for about a second I was certain I'd force it right back into my mouth, but before could make up my mind, it was crushed under my feet as I walked away.

What was the point? Nothing seemed to work and I was just waiting everybody's time. I emptied the rest of the pills into the bin and pulled out my phone. I deleted Natalie's' number, turning off my phone and turning my back on all of it. I don't need pity, or pills, I need to get away from this and do it myself. I don't last anywhere.

What if nothing is meant to last?

What if I'm not meant to last?

Part Seven:

What If I End Up Like Her?

I never went to see Natalie again. She called and called, for weeks on end but she gave up in the end, just like everybody else did. She knew she had no right to make me come back, I'd done my time 'recommended' by the hospital ages ago. Eventually, after the phone calls stopped, the letter confirming they'd removed me from their service arrived. I looked at her signature on the bottom of the page, for just a second, then threw the letter in the bin. I felt awful for my sudden departure, that I'd never said goodbye to her but I couldn't face her after disappearing like this. Something snapped inside me that day and I knew I couldn't go on living like that anymore. I didn't want to talk about my feelings, I didn't want to record how much sleep I'd had or how much I'd eaten. I didn't want to rely on pills to live, no matter how good Natalie said they would be if I'd given it a fair try.

I'd finally managed to hold onto a job for a few months, working in a disgustingly sleazy pub that mum frequented, looking for equally sleazy men to lure into bed. I couldn't count the number of times I'd finished my shift by bundling my drunken mother into a taxi and trying to keep her from vomiting until we got home. It was actually her that got me this poor excuse of a job, she practically lived there so it wasn't hard to convince the manager to hire me. She was one of the favourites, which honestly couldn't be that hard once you take a look at the type of people that stumbled into the doors as soon as it was midday.

The job was fine. The pay was minimal, but if you faked a smile and wore a skirt there were a lot of tips floating around, especially when it was getting closer to midnight and nobody could think straight. Once somebody paid me with a fifty for one drink and told me to keep the change, but that was right before he passed out on one of the pool tables.

Yesterday was my twenty-first birthday, and it started off in a way that should have been so shameful but was just routine for me now, sneaking out of somebody else's bedroom, finding my shoes and finding a bus stop. My head was fine when I crawled out from under the covers, glancing over to the man passed out next to me. He was one of the regulars, we'd hooked up a few times when I got off late and couldn't get home from work. He was pretty good-looking, I suppose. He had sandy-coloured hair that he kept up in a ponytail, even though it was currently covering the pillows, and big blue eyes. He was cute, and a very nice guy. He'd usually offer to drive me home on mornings like this but I felt like I could use the walk.

I don't know when this became normal, but it was easy. I felt wanted, even if just for a night. It was starting to get warm out, but the early mornings were still frosty so I took his jacket from the back of the door and left, jumping on the first bus home I could find. It didn't take long at all, I knew the way with my eyes closed.

'Happy birthday.' My mother said as I opened the door, trying to be quiet as possible, 'Good night last night then?' She said, raising an eyebrow. I walked over to the kettle and started making some coffee as she walked over and pushed a box into my hands. I stared at her, wondering what she was doing.

'Well, open it then!' she said, looking far too excited for this early in the morning. 'Thanks, mum?' I wasn't sure what to make of it, so I put the box on the counter and started to rip off the tape. Inside was a beautiful dress, maybe the most beautiful I'd ever seen. It was a deep red, with beautiful patterns laced into the dropping neckline. I ran my fingers over the soft material, and couldn't help but feel a smile come to my lips.

'I love it, it's beautiful. You didn't have to get me anything like this though.' I awkwardly edged in for a hug, and I felt her sigh into my shoulders, 'It's not every day my daughter turns twenty-one. I can't believe you're all grown up!' She pulled away, keeping hold of my hands and looking right at me, as though she'd just noticed I was actually here for the first time in years. She took over making the coffee and told me to go get a shower so she could take me out for breakfast. I just nodded and walked into the bathroom, letting the water wash the last night away from me.

Breakfast turned into a shopping trip for some new shoes to match my dress, and then into a quick bite for lunch. Before I knew it, we'd spent the whole day together and I needed to get to work. As I've gone to pull a pair of jeans from my wardrobe, mum swanned into the room, holding my beautiful new dress up and shaking her head. 'Evie, it's your birthday. Come on, let's go and celebrate.'

I laughed, telling her I had to work tonight but she was not taking no for an answer. I rolled my eyes and turned off my phone, letting her dress me up and do my hair before dragging me into a taxi and whisking me off into the night. I'd forgotten just how many bars there were lurking around the backstreets of town, and we were hitting all of them, laughing as we stumbled drunkenly from door to door.

We were in the fifth or sixth bar, throwing back some stupidly expensive cocktails that a couple of drunken men had bought us, when mum put her arm around me, forcing me to try and focus in on the conversation rather than watching the action unfolding around us.

'You two are so alike, I'd swear you were sisters!' the older drunkard said, leering at me in a way that made my skin crawl a little bit. 'I know!' mum shouted above the music, glowing, 'We've got a lot in common now my baby is all grown up! She's like my best friend'

I couldn't breathe. It was like all the air in the room had disappeared. The whole room was like an vacuum. It felt like my whole body had suddenly turned to ice and I could feel my eyes begin to well, tears trying to break through to the surface. I sucked in a breathe and tried to swallow back the lump that was forming in the back of my throat. Slowly standing up, I swung my handbag over my arm and told them I was popping to the bathroom before I melted into the crowd of people.

It was easy for me to slip out the smoker's door undetected and not stop until I'd reached my front door.

What did he say? We're so alike.

We have so much in common.

I'm just like her.

I can't be her.

But I've let myself turn into someone I don't want to be.

I've been so numb that I didn't even realise what was happening.

It hit me like a brick wall. This is why she suddenly took an interest in getting to know me, why she'd realised I existed at all. I had become so similar to her in a way, blocking out all of lifes problems with cheap booze and even cheaper men.

She was always passed out when the crying and screaming came, when I fell to pieces. She was only there when I could play the part of her little doll. A scream forced its way from my lungs as I slammed my fists into the wall, feeling my little finger crunch against the bricks. I'd never learned how to throw a good punch; I've only watched as I've been on the receiving end.

I tore my shoes from my feet and launched them across the room, straight through the kitchen window. I watched as the glass smashed into thousands of pieces, just like my life had been doing for so long.

I missed the time I couldn't feel a thing, because this pain was too much.

'I don't want to be like her, please!' I cried out, 'I've tried my hardest but I'm just fucked up. I can't do anything.' I slid down the wall and wiped the tears falling down my face, 'I give up.'

And those three words made all the anger and the panic seep away from my body. A sudden clarity surrounded me and my mind was calm. All the pain was ebbing away from my body, taking my will to fight with it.

I give up.

I'm done.

I know what to do.

I've been fighting with my own mind for so long, and I was tired. I needed this to stop, and I knew exactly what I needed to do. I picked myself up from the floor, wincing slightly as I leant on my broken finger. I slipped on some flat shoes and gathered all my hair from my face.

I emptied my bag out onto the kitchen side, watching the contents spill out. The screen on my phone cracked as it came into contact with the tile but I didn't stop to check if anybody had called to see where I was. I shoved the largest bottle of vodka we had into the bag and zipped it up as I walked to the door.

I turned around and looked at the place I'd spent the last twenty-one years in, covered in broken glass. It reminded me of smashed photo frames and damaged furniture, holes in walls and screaming that went on deep into the night.

There wasn't one part of this house that hadn't seen the worst of me, and there wasn't one part of me that wanted to stay around and see what it had in store next.

What if this is the end of my story?

What if this solves everything?

Part Eight:

What If I Jump?

So, that's my story.

That's how I came to be sitting on this pier, the morning after my twenty-first birthday, waiting for the tide to turn. It seems silly, to be here because of an off-handed compliment from a drunken stranger. That's what it might look like but it's not because of him, or even my mother. It was just the final piece of the puzzle for me. The final push I needed to find the solution for all my problems. I didn't even realise I'd been thinking about this for a while, but somewhere in the back of my mind, I've been planning this exact day for a long time.

I read a few years ago that a man killed himself after his toaster broke. There was a giant fuss in the media, people ridiculing this man for taking his own life because he couldn't have his breakfast. I'll admit, at the time I couldn't understand how something so small could send somebody over the edge, but now I understand him perfectly. It's like getting kicked in the head, over and over, each one hurts like hell but you can still get up and fight again, until that last kick comes in, and it puts you down for good.

It's not that single kick that breaks people, it's all the ones that come before, hurting more and more each time until eventually you just can't stand it anymore.

This is the beautiful ending to a terrible story, I suppose. I was always surrounded by noise and chaos, but right here it's peaceful. The sun is starting to peek through the clouds, and the only noise is the water as it changes direction.

It's time.

I'm tired, and now I finally get to rest. It feels like one of those Sunday mornings you read about it books, when you're blissfully sleepy and relaxed and don't have a single care in the world.

I finish the bottle, leaving it resting against one of the bars.

Like a small reminder that I was here. I look into the sky.

I take a breath, once more.

I jump.

What If this wasn't the answer?

Part Nine:

What If I Don't Want to Die?

There are no words to describe how it feels
being trapped under the waves. Being pulled
further and further away by a current I'm too
weak to fight off. Maybe I'm too weak, too
tired, but I'm also too late. My eyes sting
from the salty water, and my lungs begin to
feel like fire, filling with smoke, just
begging me to open my mouth and let it out.
I thought the water was silent, but it's
deafening, roaring like a monster and
ringing in my ears.

I close my eyes as if maybe I could wake up
back on the pier, and change my mind.
Maybe I could go home, maybe I can try
harder and maybe I can get better. Is it
possible for a human to just explode? I feel
like I could, my whole body is like a
grenade, and it's going to destroy me.

I try to move, try to force myself upwards
but the weight of the water drags me down.

This weight, the weight of dying, is heavier than anything I've carried in my life. I'm playing one thing on repeat; I don't want to die.

I don't want to die.

I can't die yet.

Please, don't let me die yet.

The world went black.

Part Ten:

What If?

I've always heard people talking about what happens right before you die. I'd never given in much thought. I didn't think there was a heaven or a hell, a day of judgement or a magical bridge to cross. You're born, you live, you die. There's nothing after death, right?

One of the most reoccurring theories I've heard is that just moments before you leave this world, you see this amazing, bright white light that is supposed to come and guide you to the next part of your afterlife, or maybe to your new one wherever that may be. They, whoever they are, also say that while you're in this calming, welcoming bright light, you'll get to see your entire life flash before your eyes, like a highlight reel to remind you of everything you've done in your life, all you've accomplished and all you're leaving behind.

My highlight reel wasn't like that at all.

It was question after question, all of the ones I'd never got to ask and would never be able to get an answer to. What if I'd fallen in love? What if I'd found my passion, my calling in life? What if I'd had my own family? What if I grew old gracefully? What if I tried harder? What if I'd tried at all? A life that I'd longer for was playing out silently in front of, showing for everything that I could have fought for if only I'd known how to. I could have tried, I could have done something instead of writing myself off as a waste of air.

Air that was running out.

These visions before me might not be real, but the one thing I know is that this light is very real.

It's so close I can feel it, warming up the edges of my body where they'd felt like ice moments before, thawing out the chill inside my chest and filling my lungs with heat. It's beautiful and clear and it looks like a glowing manifestation of hope and happiness. It wraps itself around me,

consuming every part of my mind and body,
and it feels like a surreal embrace.

Suddenly, the light is everywhere, and
everything and everyone I've ever seen.

And then finally, it's over.

Part Eleven:

What If Everything Turns Out Okay?

My Name Is Evie Jackson.

I am twenty-two years old and Gemini.

My Mother is a recovering alcoholic, and my father is slowly learning how to be my parent.

It is 4.30pm.

I am sitting in the common room of the rehabilitation centre with my doctor.

And I almost died last year.

I stole a bottle of Vodka from my mother, jumped into a river and almost drowned to death.

If it hadn't been some for a stranger in a fast car who'd seen me trespassing, the police wouldn't have come.

And if the police hadn't come, nobody would have been there to pull me out of water.

I wouldn't be here to tell this story.

All of the questions and 'What Ifs?' that led to that jump have stayed with me, but so have the ones I found under the waves. But now there are new questions that I realise I want the answers to.

What if we find Dad and explain? What if I reach out to Isla and tell her I love her? What If I ask Natalie to take me back? What if I get mum some help to get sober?

I've found a way to turn all these questions into goals, into dreams. To new places I can focus my tired mind on and find a small glimmer of hope. It's not an easy journey, some nights I find myself wishing for a wave to come and swallow me, but I'm learning to swim. I don't know if I'll ever really recover from the last twenty-two years of my life but I am going to try.

I've been given a second chance to live, and I am going to live it as well as I can.

It'll be hard.

It'll hurt.

It'll keep me up at nights and make me cry about things I've tried not to think about.

But it's worth it.

After all, what if everything turns out just fine?

The End, For Now.

Acknowlegments

They say there's a story in every one of us, and I'm lucky enough to have people around me who have shaped my story into something very different that it could have been.

Thank you to Joe, my oldest friend and the first person to ever read this book back when it was just a few pages of rambling nonsense.

Tyler, for the endless supply of support and wine.

Special mention to the most amazing writers group in the world, Bethany Club, for all the help and love.

And if you're reading this, thank you! Thank you for helping me make this possible!

Printed in Great Britain
by Amazon

65884791R00058